15 MINUTE
WAIT AT
THIS POINT ↓

For my editor, Emily

Published by Roaring Brook Press
Roaring Brook Press is a division of Holtzbrinck Publishing Holdings Limited Partnership
120 Broadway, New York, NY 10271
mackids.com

Library of Congress Control Number: 2020908949

ISBN: 978-1-250-23254-0

Our books may be purchased in bulk for promotional, educational, or business use.
Please contact your local bookseller or the Macmillan Corporate and Premium Sales
Department at (800) 221-7945 ext. 5442 or by email
at MacmillanSpecialMarkets@macmillan.com.

First edition, 2020
Art direction by Jen Keenan

Printed in China by 1010 Printing International Limited, North Point, Hong Kong

1 3 5 7 9 10 8 6 4 2

TWO MANY BIRDS

by CINDY DERBY

Roaring Brook Press
New York

TICKETS

MAXIMUM
OCCUPANCY
100 BIRDS

TICKETS
NO RUNNING

MAXIMUM
OCCUPANCY
100 BIRDS

ICKETS

NO RUNNING

MAXIMUM
OCCUPANCY
100 BIRDS

NO YELLING!
02

MAXIMUM
OCCUPANCY
100 BIRDS

HEY! NO FLUFFIN' THE FEATHERS!
13
hair MUST NOT PASS THIS LINE

MAXIMUM
OCCUPANCY
100 BIRDS

34
NO NESTING!

NO RESTING!

NO HAIR GEL!

NO NUDITY!!!

NO PESTING!

68

NO BLINKING!

NO POOPING ON THE GROUND!!!!!!

93

NO MORE BIRDS ALLOWED!

NO PARROTS ON TUESDAYS
NO LONG HAIRS
MAXIMUM OCCUPANCY 100 BIRDS
NO BIRD BATHS
NO DIAPERS (USE POTTY)
BIRDA-POTTY

AND QUIT YOUR CRACKLING!
At Lunch
be back:
IN 5 MINUTES!

V.I.B.
SECTION
ACORN
LUNCH

CRAAAAAAACK!

ACORN LUNCH
V.I.B. SECTION
At Lunch be back: IN 5 MINUTES!
102

NO CLIPPING TOENAILS
NO PARROTS ON TUESDAYS
WEDNESDAYS THURSDAYS FRIDAYS
NO FAKE MUSTACHES
NO LONG HAIRS
MAXIMUM OCCUPANCY 100 BIRDS
NO BIRD BATHS
NO LAUGHING
NO DIAPERS (USE POTTY)
BIRDA-POTTY

TWO
MANY
BIRDS!!!

102

NO CLIPPING TOENAILS
NO PARROTS ON TUESDAYS
WEDNESDAYS THURSDAYS FRIDAYS SATURDAYS
NO FAKE MUSTACHES
NO LONG HAIRS
MAXIMUM OCCUPANCY 100 BIRDS
NO BIRD BATHS
NO LAUGHING
NO DIAPERS (USE POTTY)
BIRDA-POTTY

NO FAKE MUSTACHES
NO PARROTS ON
SATURDAYS
NO
TOENAILS
MAXIMUM OCCUPANCY 100 BIRDS 50000
NO BIRD BATHS
NO
NO DIAPERS (USE POTTY)
BIRDA-POTTY

HEY!
HEY!
HEY!
HEY!
HEY!
HEY!
HEY!

NO NETS!

NO WORMS!

NO TRESPASSING!
NO WORM ZONE
NO HOLES!
NO WIGGLE ROOM!

ACORN DINNER

ACORN DINNER

ACORN DINNER

NO THANKS

ACORN DINNER

ACORN DINNER
NO RAINING
ACORN DINNER

ACORN

NO...
GROWING?

A-OK
ACORN

HEY!
STILL TOO
MANY BIRDS!

NO CROWDING
NO WORMS ON TUESDAYS
NO STEPPING ON THE LITTLE ONES

NO OVER WATERING
2 weeks old

ATTENTION, BIRDS!

NO MORE WAITING!

GRAND OPENING
NO SHIRTS NO SHOES NO PROBLEM
Welcome center
MAPS, INFO, and TOURS
THIS TREE is 1 YEAR OLD
Missing DIAPER